THE COMPLETE ADVENTURES OF
The Mole Sisters

The Mole Sisters series

THE COMPLETE ADVENTURES OF
The Mole Sisters

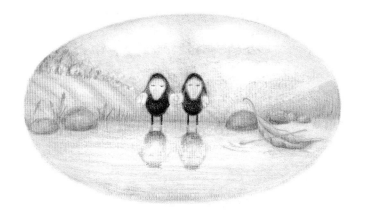

Ten stories written and illustrated by Roslyn Schwartz

Annick Press Ltd.
Toronto • New York • Vancouver

Contents

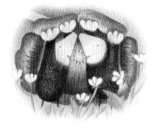

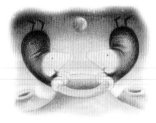

To Barb
—R.S.

"All good stuff," said the mole sisters.

The Mole Sisters
and the Busy Bees

"Sometimes it's important to do nothing," said the mole sisters.

And that's what they
were doing ...

under the tree

when along came a bee.

Bzzzzzzzzzzzz.

"Busy busy busy,"
said the bee.

"What are you doing?"
asked the mole sisters.

"Can't stop," replied the
bee. "Too busy."

"Not us!" said the
mole sisters.

And they followed him
out of the forest,

through the tall grass,

and into a meadow
full of flowers.

"How lovely," said the
mole sisters.

"Mmmm."

"Sniff-sniff."

"Mumble-bumble."

"BOO!!"

"Now we're as busy as bees!"   "And we look like flowers!"

Buzz Buzz Buzz Buzz

"They think we're flowers too!"

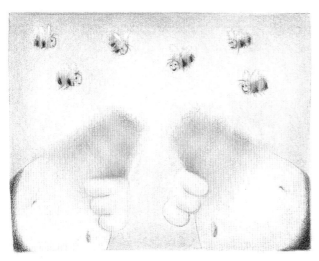

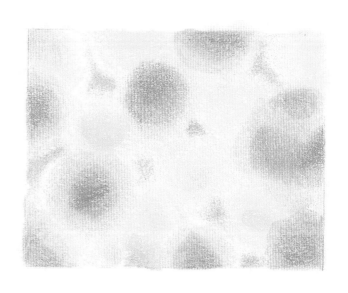

"AH-AH-AH———   *TISHOOOO!"*

"Bless you," said the bees.

"Thank you," said the mole sisters.

And they went back
to doing nothing,

just as they started out to do.

The Mole Sisters
and the Rainy Day

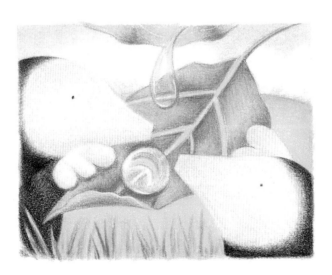

"What a lovely day," said
the mole sisters.

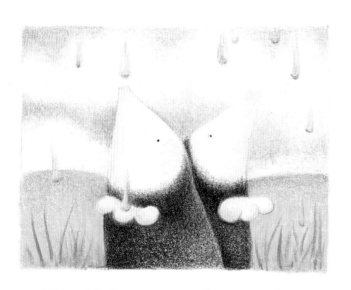

Until it started to rain.

"Never mind," they said.

"It won't last."

But it did.

WHOOSH

"Yikes!"

Down their hole they went.   KERPLUNK

"Hey?"

"Uh-oh."

"Never mind," they said.
"It won't last."

But it did.

"Now what?"

"Of course."

"Well done."

"Tum, Tee, Tum, Tee Ta ..."

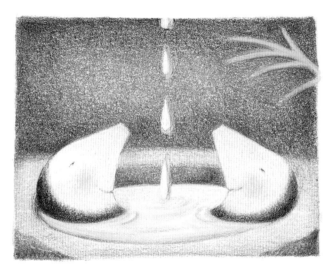

"Perfect."

And they splished

and splashed

until the sun came out

and the rain stopped.

"See?"

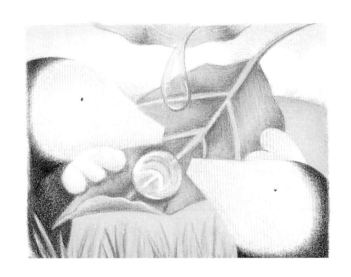

"We were right."

"It didn't last long after all."

"What a lovely day," said
the mole sisters.

And it was!

The Mole Sisters
and the Fairy Ring

"Look!" said the mole sisters.

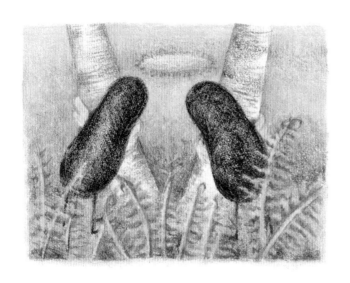

"Over there."

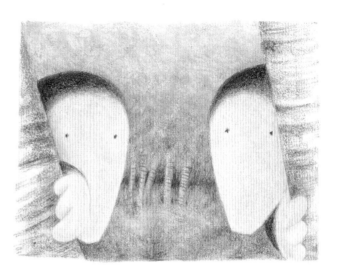

"See?"

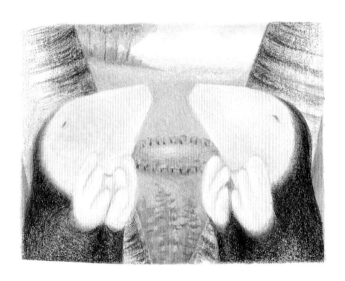

"It's a ... it's a ..."

"Fairy ring!"

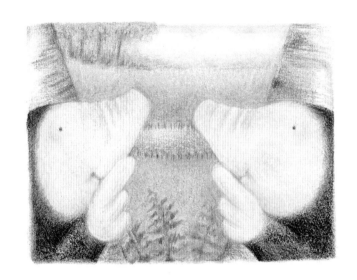

"Sssssh."

"The fairies don't know
we're here."

"Let's sneak up on them."   "Hee hee, sneak sneak."

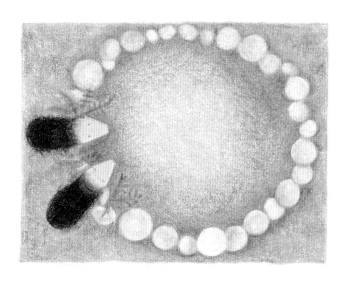

"Oh!"

"No one home."

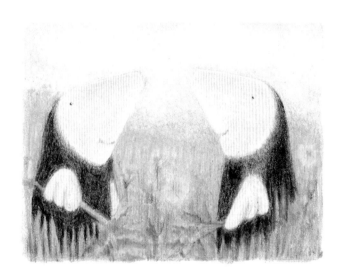

"Never mind," said the
mole sisters.

"Let's be fairies!"

"Okey-dokey."

"How do we look?"

"All we need is fairy dust ..."

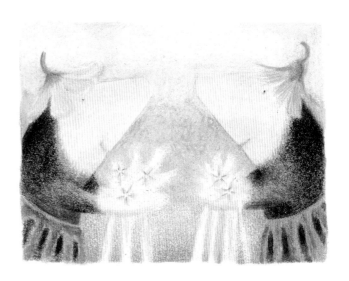

Twinkle twinkle

"... and *voilà!*"

"We look just like fairies!"

Flit flit

Whizz

Bang.

Whoomph!

"Whew."

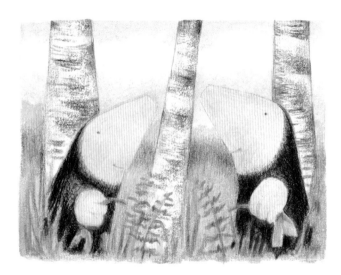

"Enough of that,"
said the mole sisters.

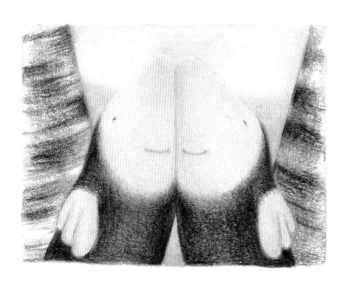

"Let's be moles."   And they were!

The Mole Sisters
and the Moonlit Night

The world is a wonderful place

and anything can happen

on a beautiful
moonlit night.

"La bella luna," sang the
mole sisters in Italian,

and gazed up at the
night sky.

"Oh look!"

"A shooting star."

"Quick—let's make a wish."   "Mmmm ...

... mmmmm ...

MWAH—it worked!"

"We're on the moon."

"Imagine that!
Moles on the moon."

"It's a bit like home,"
they said,

and sighed.

"The world really is
a wonderful place."

"*Look!!*"

"There it is again."

"*Quick*—
let's make another wish."

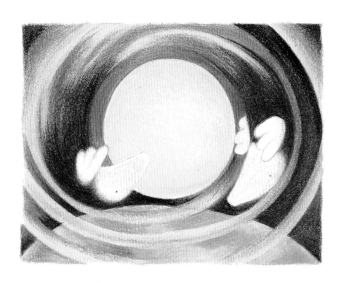

"Mmmmmm ...   MWAH—it worked!"

"We're home."

"And ...

... that just goes to show," said the mole sisters.

"Anything really can happen

on a beautiful moonlit night.   Especially to us!"

The Mole Sisters
and the Piece of Moss

The mole sisters live in a
hole under the ground.

But not all the time.

That would be dull.

And the mole sisters are
never dull.

"Not like me," said the
piece of moss.

"Nonsense," said the
mole sisters.

"You're lovely."

BOINGA-BOINGA

"Come with us."

"Aooh, how exciting," said
the piece of moss.

"Never a dull moment,"
said the mole sisters.

"Especially here ...   on top of the world!"

"Goodbye then," said the
mole sisters. "We have to
go home now."

"Ready?"

"Set?"

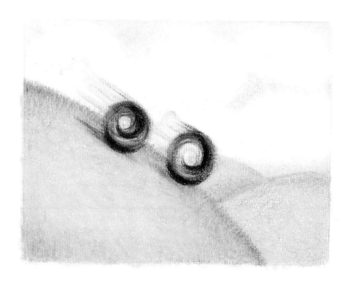

"Go!"

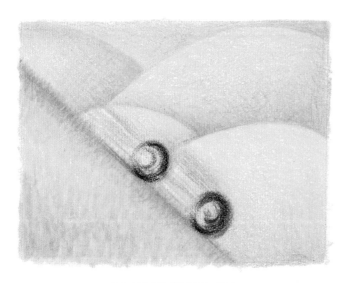

WHEEEEE

"Where are we?"

"Here we are!"
said the mole sisters.

"Hee Hee Hee Hee ..."

They laughed until the
sun set

and the stars came out.

"They're so pretty ...   ... just like us."

"Down we go then."

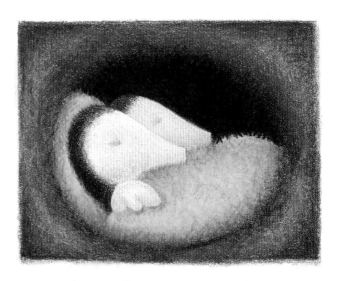

Good night, sweet dreams.

The Mole Sisters
and the Wavy Wheat

"Which way?"
said the mole sisters.

"We always go left ..."

So they went right
instead.

"Just for a change!"

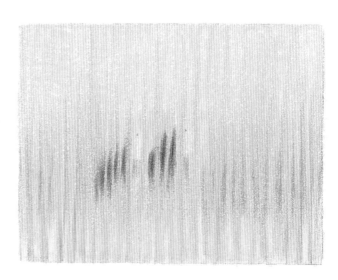

"Now which way?" said
the mole sisters.

"Hmmm—

UP!"

So up they went ...   all the way to the top.

Oh dear.

"Yoohoo!"

"YOOHOOOO!!"

"Let's go this way."

Oops.

"Which way now?"
said the mole sisters.

"Yikes … hold on!"

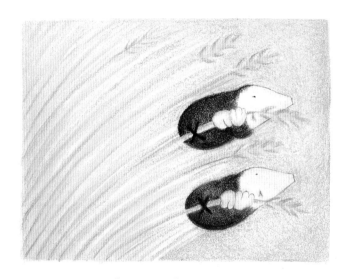

Swish to the right—

swish to the left— one, two, three and …

"DOWN!"

The mole sisters
waved goodbye to
thc wavy wheat

and marched left
right left right

all the way home.

Then they swept the mole
hole up down, up down.

"Now we've been
everywhere," said the
mole sisters.

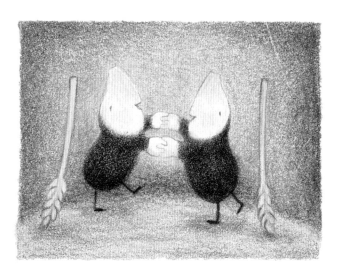

"Everywhere except bed."

'Night 'Night.

The Mole Sisters
and the Blue Egg

The mole sisters were
looking for something.

But what?

"We don't know," they said.

"We'll know it when
we see it."

"Ooooooooooo."

"Aaaaaaaah."

Is this it?

"You never know,"
they said.

Never know what?

"Well ...   ... !"

"You never know," said
the mole sisters,

"till you try!"

Try what?

"Everything."

"Tweet tweet."

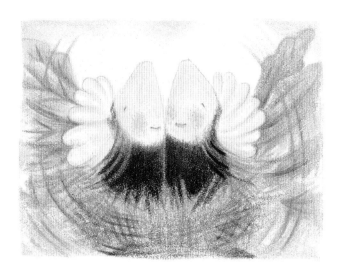

"Flap flap."

"All good stuff."

"See?" said the mole sisters.

"Alley-oop."

WHEEEEEEEEE

WHOOOOOOOSH

PLONK!

"Look!"

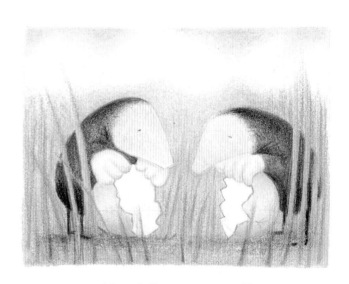

"A blue egg."

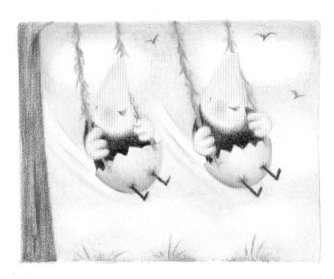

"Now we know what we're looking for," said the mole sisters.

"And we've found it, too!"

The Mole Sisters
and the Cool Breeze

"Hot," said the mole sisters.

"Very."

"What we need …

… is a nice cool breeze."

"Breeze?" said the
dandelion.

"What breeze?

We haven't had a breeze for weeks."

"Oh," said the mole
sisters. "Pity."

And they started to fan
themselves.

Swoosh swoosh

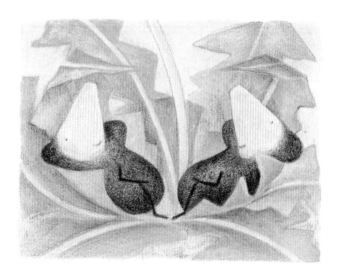

"Most refreshing."

"Ahem," said the dandelion.
"What about me?"

"Wait a minute," said the
mole sisters.

Swoosh swoosh

"That's better," said
the dandelion.

"What about us?"
cried the others.

"Shall we?" said the
mole sisters.

"Here we go."

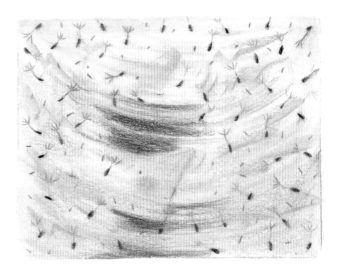

Swoosh swoosh

"That's better," said
the dandelions.

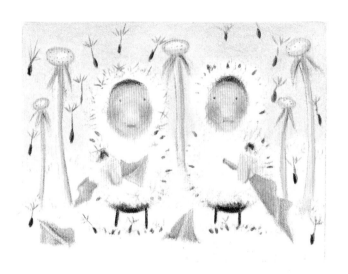

"But not for us!" said the
mole sisters.

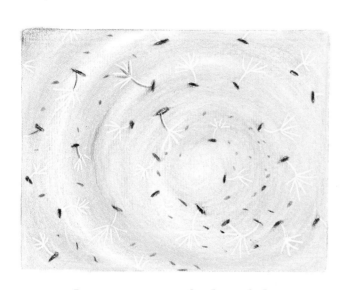

Then out of the blue
came a breeze.

"Aaah," said the mole sisters.

"That's better."

"It's just what we needed."

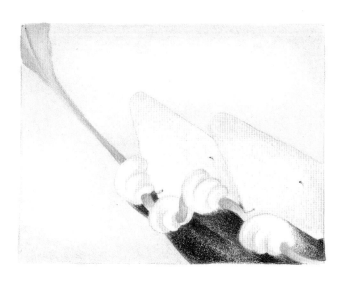

Swoosh swoosh

"A nice cool breeze."

The Mole Sisters
and the Question

The mole sisters were thinking.

"Who are we?" "Good question," they said.

"Let's see."

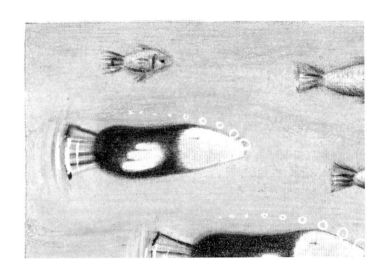

"Are we fish?"

"Maybe."

"But fish live in water …

... and we don't."

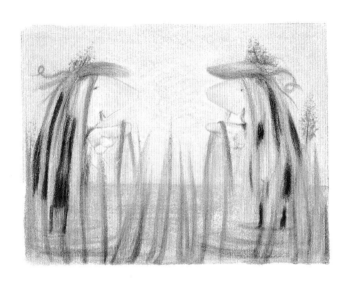

"Hee hee."

"Brrrrrrrr."

"Then we're not fish."

"Are we birds?" said the
mole sisters.

"Birds fly."

Wiggle wiggle

Quack quack

"Not us."

"Then we're not birds,"
said the mole sisters.

"Cooo-eee."

"Are we snails?"

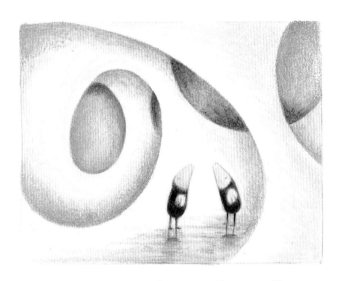

"Snails live alone."

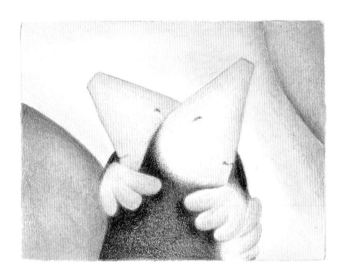

"We could never do that."

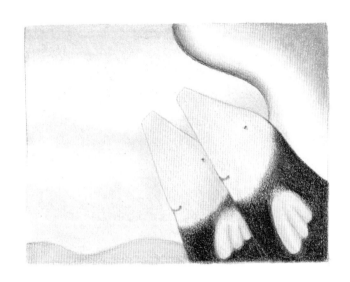 

"Then lucky we're not snails," said the mole sisters.

"But if we're not snails, birds, or fish ...

… who are we?"

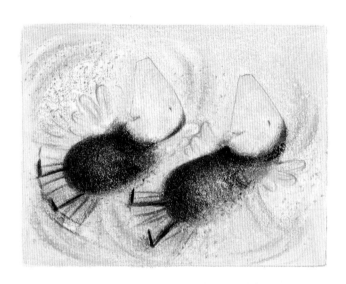

"Hee hee hee."

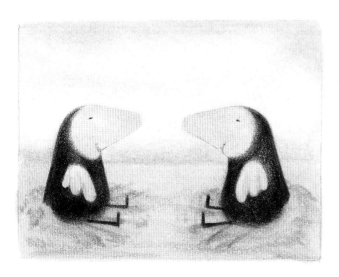

"We're the mole sisters, of course!"

And that was enough thinking for one day.

The Mole Sisters
and the Way Home

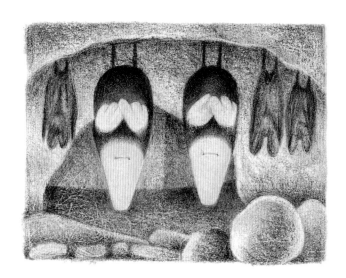

The mole sisters were on
their way home ...

... when it started to snow.

"Oooooo."

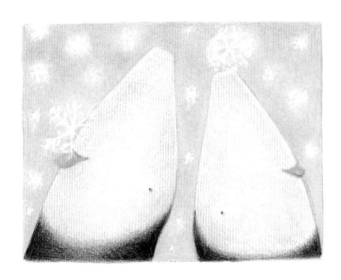

"Aaaaah," they said.

"What fun!"

"Hey ho."

"On we go."

So on they went.

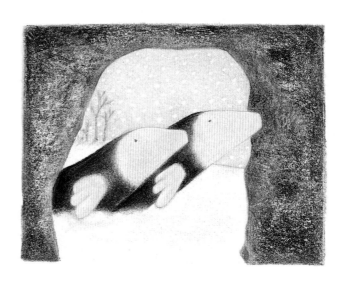

"Hmmm."

"What have we here?"

Squeak squeak

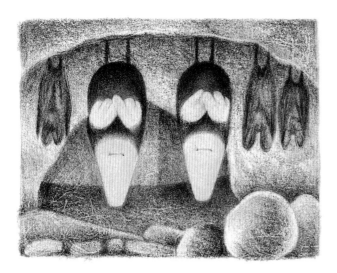

"Ups-a-daisy."

"How exciting."

"Yes indeedy."

"We've never been this way before."

"Oooooo."

"Aaaaah."

"How interesting,"
said the mole sisters.

"Very."

"Everyone's here."

"But where are *we*?"

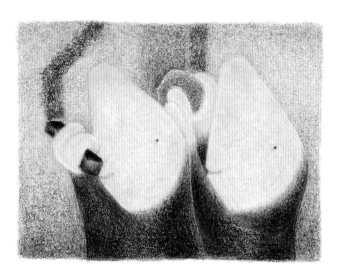

"Just a minute ..."   "There we are!"

"Now on we go,"
said the mole sisters.

"Hey ho."

And on they went ...

all the way home.

Originally published individually by Annick Press Ltd.
© Roslyn Schwartz (text and illustrations)—The Mole Sisters and the Rainy Day 1999
© Roslyn Schwartz (text and illustrations)—The Mole Sisters and the Piece of Moss 1999
© Roslyn Schwartz (text and illustrations)—The Mole Sisters and the Busy Bees 2000
© Roslyn Schwartz (text and illustrations)—The Mole Sisters and the Wavy Wheat 2000
© Roslyn Schwartz (text and illustrations)—The Mole Sisters and the Moonlit Night 2001
© Roslyn Schwartz (text and illustrations)—The Mole Sisters and the Blue Egg 2001
© Roslyn Schwartz (text and illustrations)—The Mole Sisters and the Cool Breeze 2002
© Roslyn Schwartz (text and illustrations)—The Mole Sisters and the Question 2002
© Roslyn Schwartz (text and illustrations)—The Mole Sisters and the Fairy Ring 2003
© Roslyn Schwartz (text and illustrations)—The Mole Sisters and the Way Home 2003

We acknowledge the support of the Canada Council for the Arts, the Ontario Arts Council,
and the Government of Canada through the Canada Book Fund (CBF) for our publishing
activities.

ONTARIO ARTS COUNCIL
CONSEIL DES ARTS DE L'ONTARIO

Cataloging in Publication

Schwartz, Roslyn, 1951-
    The complete adventures of the mole sisters : ten stories / written and
illustrated by Roslyn Schwartz.

(The mole sisters series)
ISBN 1-55037-883-X

    1. Moles (Animals)—Juvenile fiction. I. Title. II. Series: Schwartz, Roslyn,
1951- . Mole sisters series.

PS8587.C5785C65 2004   jC813'.54   C2004-902262-8

The art in this book was rendered in colored pencils.
The text was typeset in Apollo.

Distributed in Canada by:
Firefly Books Ltd.
50 Staples Avenue, Unit 1
Richmond Hill, ON
L4B 0A7

Published in the U.S.A. by Annick Press (U.S.) Ltd.
Distributed in the U.S.A. by:
Firefly Books (U.S.) Inc.
P.O. Box 1338
Ellicott Station
Buffalo, NY 14205

Printed in China

Also available in e-book format. Please visit
www.annickpress.com/ebooks for more details. Or scan

Visit us at: www.annickpress.com